T0392312

The Curry Kid Explores India:

One Smart Cookie and the Wonders of the World

Written by **Jayanthi Gaspar**

Illustrations by **Rick Sanders**

To order additional copies of this book, contact:
Xlibris
1-888-795-4274
www.Xlibris.com
Orders@Xlibris.com

ISBN: Softcover 978-1-7960-5483-5
Hardcover 978-1-7960-5484-2
EBook 978-1-7960-5482-8

Print information available on the last page

Rev. date: 09/20/2019

To Julian, Philip, Jeremy,
Lauren, and Baylee for their
encouragement and support.

In loving memory of
Jeremy Gaspar
1985-2017

New Delhi
INDIA

In a faraway land of India lived a sweet Indian couple. They were happy and content in their little home. One day when they were visiting with friends, they heard about a gingerbread cookie, shaped like a person, that kept running away from its baker. Now, the couple wondered how this could be. They wanted to see for themselves. So they decided to bake a gingerbread cookie of their own.

After finding the perfect gingerbread cookie recipe, they got right to baking. They followed the recipe as directed, but they also added a few Indian ingredients, like curry powder, cumin seeds, and cardamom. The dough was sweet and savory. They reminded themselves to pay close attention to the last tip: *Do not open the oven until the timer goes off!*

They shaped the dough into the cutest boy. They decorated him with raisin eyes, dried red chili for the mouth, cardamom buttons, ginger shoes, and saffron hair. They wrapped licorice around his head to form a turban hat, placing a pomegranate seed in the middle of his hat as the jewel. He was finally ready to go into the oven, and the timer was set.

While the woman went out to the garden to tend to her flowers, curiosity got the best of the man. The oven timer had not yet gone off. *Maybe the timer is broken*, he thought. He tried to keep his mind busy by reading a book, but his eyes kept going back to the oven. “Surely, no cookie can come to life,” he muttered. He opened the oven door ever so slowly . . .

And out popped the cookie, making a dash straight for the front door.

The man tried to grab the cookie, but it was already outside, running fast. The woman tried to grab the cookie as it swung past her in the garden, but she missed. They shouted at the cookie, "Come back, come back!"

The cookie said, "I'm the Curry Kid, fast as can be. You can try, but you won't catch me."

"Stop!" cried the couple. "We want to have you for tea time!"

The Curry Kid saw the beauty of the land in front of him and instantly decided that he wanted to travel the world—and not get eaten! He kept running as he shouted back to the couple, "I don't have time for tea. I have so much land to see!"

Once he was certain that he was safe, he slowed down to enjoy the sights. Along the way, he almost bumped into the biggest bird he had ever seen: a glorious peacock!

The minute the beautiful bird saw the yummy cookie, it opened its feathers and danced in front of the Curry Kid, trying to distract him.

The Curry Kid thought that was quite fascinating, until the peacock opened its mouth, preparing to take a chomp out of him!

But this was one smart cookie. He took off running again, chanting, "I'm the Curry Kid, fast as can be.
You can try, but you won't catch me."

"Stop!" cried peacock. "Don't you want to admire my feathers?"

The Curry Kid shouted back, "I don't have time to admire peacock feathers or stay for tea.
I have so much land to see!"

When he came around the bend, he almost tripped over a sacred cow relaxing in the field. The startled cow got a scent of the cookie, much more appealing than eating hay!

“Stop!” said the cow. “You can’t just run past me. I deserve some respect!”

The Curry Kid wanted to pay respect, but he knew what to expect! So, he kept on his way as he yelled:

“I’m the Curry Kid, fast as can be. You can try, but you won’t catch me.”

“Stop!” cried the sacred cow.

The Curry Kid shouted back, “I don’t have time to respect sacred cows, admire peacock feathers, or stay for tea. I have so much land to see!”

As the Curry Kid was running, he came across monkeys hanging around a Hindu temple, eating food fed to them by the people. The mischievous monkeys knew a good thing when they saw one. The monkeys tried to grab the cookie and take a bite.

Just like the monkeys knew a good thing, Curry Kid knew a bad thing! So he didn't even bother to stop and kept on going as he yelled:

"I'm the Curry Kid, fast as can be. You can try, but you won't catch me."

The monkeys cried, "Feed us! Feed us!"

The Curry Kid shouted back, "I don't have time to feed monkeys, give respect to sacred cows, admire peacock feathers, or stay for tea.

I have so much land to see!"

Just as he went around the corner, he heard music and saw a classical Indian dancer performing. He took just a small break to enjoy the performance, when suddenly, the dancer saw him and stopped dancing. She said, "Namaste!" which means hello in Hindi, an Indian language. "I am so famished from all this dancing! Please stop, so I can just get a good whiff of you."

The Curry Kid knew better than to take that risk. He hopped up and ran away.

"I'm the Curry Kid, fast as can be. You can try, but you won't catch me."

The dancer, with her nose up in the air, abandoned the performance and ran after the cookie, yelling, "Namaste, cookie! Stop, so I can get one more good smell, please!

The Curry Kid shouted back, "I will not get too close to a classical dancer for her to take another whiff, feed monkeys, give respect to sacred cows, admire peacock feathers, or stay for tea. I have so much land to see!

ദേവീ ശരണം

Suddenly, he felt the ground shake beneath his feet. A huge animal was running after him—an elephant, to be exact. The Curry Kid just knew he was a goner; there was no way to outrun this enormous animal.

The elephant bellowed, "Don't be afraid of me. I'm a gentle animal. People stand in long lines and pay to ride on me. I could give you one for free."

The Curry Kid thought, *I could get a free ride, and you would get a free cookie.*

Shaking his head and backing away, he said to the elephant, "I'm the Curry Kid, fast as can be. You can try, but you won't catch me."

The enormous elephant ran after him, yelling, "Free ride! Free ride!"

The Curry Kid shouted back, "I don't have time for a free elephant ride. I will not get too close to a classical dancer for her to take a another whiff, feed monkeys, give respect to sacred cows, admire peacock feathers, or stay for tea. I have so much land to see!"

RJ-15
नगरीय PA-0196 सेवा

By this point, the Curry Kid was getting tired, but he was afraid to stop. To make matters worse, he was now in the middle of a busy street, with cars, trucks, and motorcycles coming from every direction! He worried this would be the end of him—either as a tasty treat or as a bunch of crumbs beneath some tires.

Then he heard a voice. It was a man in an auto rickshaw (a motorized tricycle). He told the Curry Kid to hop in and promised to take him to a safe spot. Now, the Curry Kid was suspicioius—that driver was licking his lips! It was tiffin time (a midday meal).

The Curry Kid saw no other choice but to hop in, and he took a big leap. Instead of going inside the rickshaw, he went straight on top of its roof. The driver didn't seem to mind, and away they went.

This is the bumpiest ride ever, thought the Curry Kid. He held on as best he could, knowing all his admirers were probably still trying to catch up to him.

The driver hit a big bump in the road, and the Curry Kid went flying into the air, landing right smack on top of a bush in front of a massive building of white marble in the city of Agra. He admired the magnificent structure, even though he knew he should just keep going. He wanted to know more about the building.

He saw a tour guide leading a group of people, so he joined in to see, listen, and learn. He was fascinated by all that he heard. This building was one of the Wonders of the World, the tour guide had said.

The Curry Kid had to agree. It was indeed a wonder.

Then he started to think about the other Wonders of the World.
What were they?
Where were they?
How would he get to them?

The Curry Kid went back to his running, trying to figure out how to make his dreams come true and see the rest of the Wonders of the World.

He stopped short when he ran into a white animal with black stripes. And sharp teeth! A Bengal tiger!

Oh no, thought the Curry Kid as he backed away.

The Bengal tiger smiled a toothy grin and said, “Seems like you need to get somewhere fast. Hop on my back, and we’ll flee quickly to wherever you wish to be. The jungle perhaps? You’ll be safe there and we can become . . . friends.”

The Curry Kid wanted to believe what the Bengal tiger said, but something told him to beware. Those teeth were sharp for a reason. The Curry Kid had to think fast.

How would he get himself out of this mess?

The Curry Kid came up with a plan. He asked the tiger to take him to a river near the jungle, so he could get a drink of water. The tiger agreed.

As they reached the river, he could see a boat slowly moving toward the ocean. He knew he had to stay clear of the water if he wanted to stay alive and not become a soggy mess.

So with all his strength, he took the biggest leap ever . . . and landed in the boat.

When the Bengal tiger realized he was tricked, he roared angrily from the river bank.

The Curry Kid just smiled and waved goodbye.

As the Curry Kid settled into the boat, he felt safe for the very first time in his short life.

As the boat drifted toward the ocean, he dreamt of other countries and other Wonders of the World . . .

Where would his next stop be?

About This Series

Everyone loves the old, old story of the Gingerbread Man. Teacher and author Jayanthi Gaspar decided to modify and expand that whimsical idea with the Curry Kid series, about a cookie who travels to see the Wonders of the World.

There are many categories of "wonders of the world." There are the Seven Wonders of the Ancient World, the Seven Wonders of the Natural World, and so on. This series uses the New7Wonders model regarding the most amazing monuments on Earth. The Great Pyramid of Giza in Egypt was given honorary status and added to this list because it is the only monument still in existence from the Seven Wonders of the Ancient World, and the oldest of all! The wonders in this series include:

Taj Mahal (India)
Great Pyramid of Giza (Egypt)
Petra (Jordan)
Roman Colosseum (Italy)
Chichen Itza (Mexico)
Christ the Redeemer Statue (Brazil)
Machu Picchu (Peru)
Great Wall of China (China)

We hope you will enjoy this fun twist on an old tale while learning about these magnificent monuments. At the back of each book is a glossary that further explains some of the animals, people, vehicles, and other artifacts most noted with the geographical area featured in the book.

The Curry Kid's Route

Up Next: Egypt

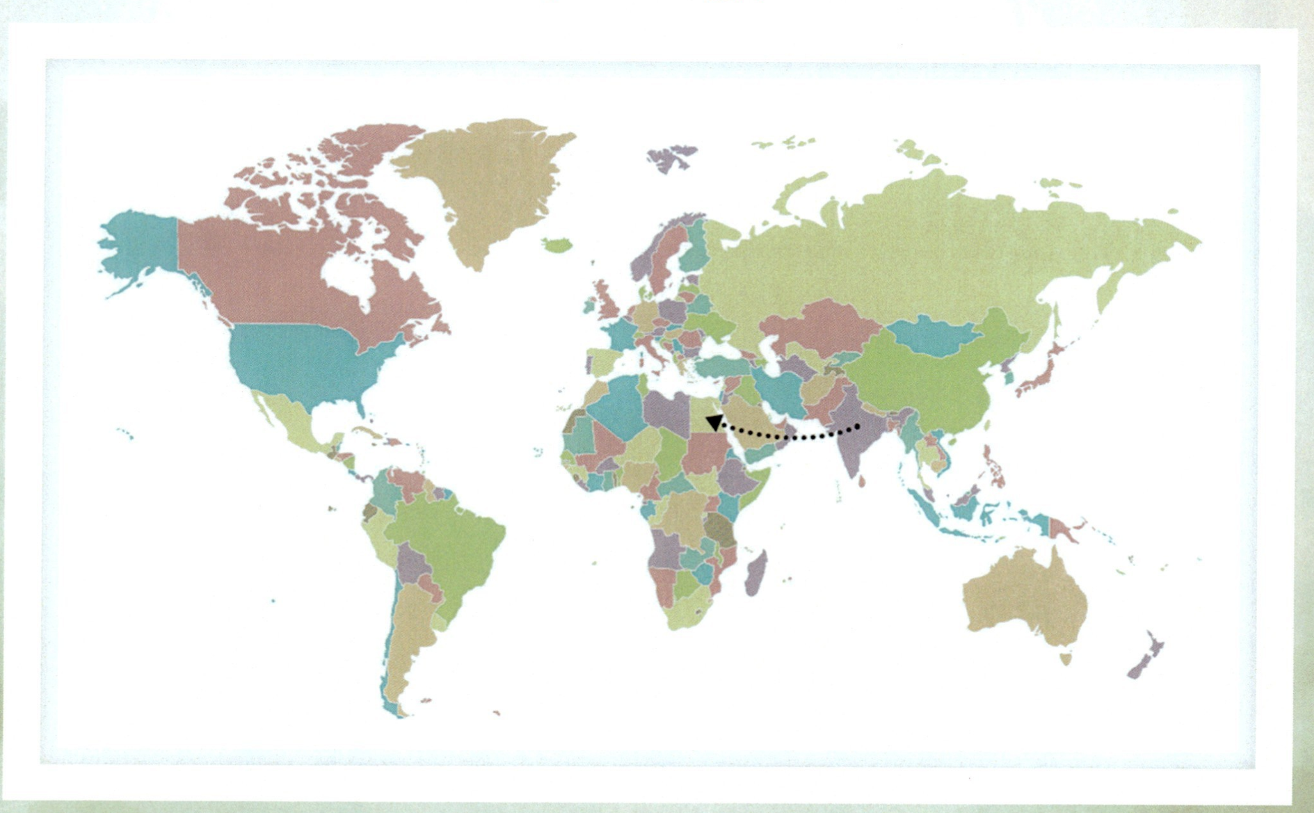

Glossary

The **peacock**, is the national bird of India. It is a symbol of grace, joy, beauty, and love. The peacock is a large and majestic bird. The males have brilliantly colored tail feathers shaped like a fan.

In India, the **cow** is a sacred animal and deeply respected. Hindus worship cows and hold them in high esteem. The reason has to do with the cows' agricultural value and their gentle nature.

Thirteen species of monkeys can be found in India. The **Rhesus Macaque** is an old-world monkey. These monkeys can be either gray or brown, and they will usually have a pink face and a long tail.

Glossary

Bharatanatyam is an **Indian classical dance**. A sophisticated vocabulary of sign language based on gestures of hands, eyes, and face muscles. The dance is accompanied by music and a singer.

Elephants are not only a cultural icon in India and throughout Asia, they also help to maintain the integrity of their forest and grassland habitats.

An **auto rickshaw** is a motorized development of the traditional pulled rickshaw or cycle rickshaw. Most have three wheels. The auto rickshaw is a common form of urban transport.

Glossary

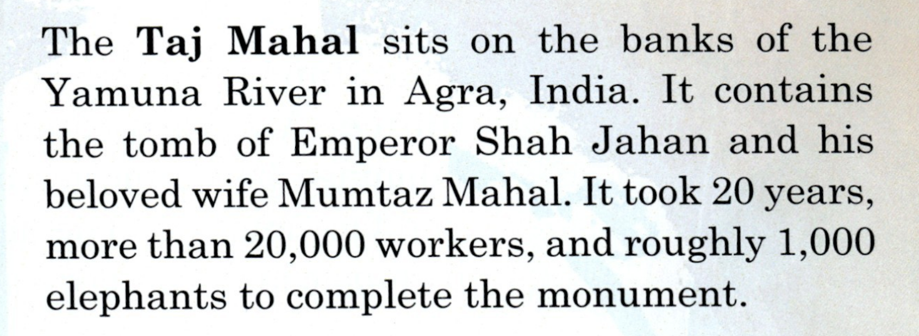

The **Taj Mahal** sits on the banks of the Yamuna River in Agra, India. It contains the tomb of Emperor Shah Jahan and his beloved wife Mumtaz Mahal. It took 20 years, more than 20,000 workers, and roughly 1,000 elephants to complete the monument.

White Bengal tigers are also called Indian tigers. They were the most numerous in population than any other tiger subspecies. White Bengal tigers were killed for sport by Indian and British royalties. As a result, their numbers declined at a fast rate until India's independence in 1947.

I appreciate the support of Philip Gaspar, Charly Stagg, my family and friends for their guidance during this venture. Finally, this book would not have been possible without the splendid support of the team at Xlibris, my publisher. I especially want to thank Janet, Rick, and Robin for putting their heads together to coordinate, illustrate, and design this book, setting the vision for future books in the series.

— Jayanthi

The Author

Jayanthi Gaspar is a recently retired elementary school teacher from College Station ISD in Texas, where she taught for twenty-two years of her twenty-six year career.

Interestingly, Jayanthi's love for writing and learning began in her own elementary-school years. Her teacher would post magazine pictures on the board and ask the students to create their own stories. Young Jayanthi enjoyed this exercise very much, getting positive feedback from her teacher and peers.

Jayanthi's path to becoming a teacher was a natural fit for her. As a published children's book author, this trend continues, as she seeks to teach and inspire through her writing and experiences with world travel.

Having traveled widely, she now wants to share and infuse the growing global mindset with the emerging generation of students. Since her retirement, she has dedicated her effort to pursue her passion for writing about our increasingly interdependent world. *The Curry Kid Explores India* is her debut children's book, the first book in her *Wonders of the World* series. One smart cookie, the Curry Kid travels to the various Wonders of the World, where he will learn about the unique cultures of each area, as well as meet some exciting new characters. Through her books, she hopes to spark an early interest in the world around us and to reach children who may not get the chance to visit other countries and learn about their cultures except through books.

Jayanthi is a mother of two sons, Philip (a doctor of podiatry) and Jeremy (a doctor of internal medicine). Her husband, Julian, is a professor of international finance at Texas A&M University in College Station, Texas.

The Illustrator

Rick Sanders has been creating art since he was a child, and he got his first camera when he was only seven years old. He earned a masters degree in art education in 1985, which led him to become proficient in a variety of media in order to teach art. He has taught students from preschools to colleges and adult education. His two great loves as an artist are oil painting and photography, but he also excels in pastels, pen-and-ink, charcoal, colored-pencil drawing, and mixed media.

He has shown his work across the United States and is an award-winning artist. Copies of his artwork have been distributed worldwide.

Rick has written for years and published *Strange Times in Yeehaw Junction* and *The Walking Bridge*. Now he also uses his imagination to paint pictures with words.

Printed in the United States
By Bookmasters